# FROGGY'S WORST PLAYDATE

# FROGGY'S WORST PLAYDATE

by JONATHAN LONDON

illustrated by FRANK REMKIEWICZ

SCHOLASTIC INC.

For Sean & Steph, Aaron, Annie, and especially for Eli
    —J.L.
For Anthony, Austin, Alex, Zack, and Jack
    —F.R.

ISBN 978-0-545-64464-8

12 11 10 9 8 7 6 5 4 3 2 1                    13 14 15 16 17 18/0

Printed in the U.S.A.                                              40

First Scholastic printing, September 2013

Set in Kabel

The illustrations for this book were rendered in watercolor and colored pencil.

It was Saturday.
Froggy woke up
and yelled, "Hurray!
It's Saturday!
I want to go out and play!"

Froggy hopped out of bed
and got dressed—*zip! zoop! zup!*
*zut! zut! zut! zat!*

Then he flopped to the kitchen for something to eat—*flop flop flop.*

He looked in the fridge—
*slam!*
He looked in the cabinet—
*slam!*
He looked in the cookie jar:
"Ah ha!"
And he ate a chocolate fly
cookie—
　　　*munch crunch munch.*

**FRROOGGYY!**

called his mother.
"Wha-a-a-t?"
"Go back to sleep, dear!
It's Saturday!
No school today!"
"I don't want to go back to sleep!" cried Froggy.
"I want to go out and play!"

So Froggy flopped over to
Max's house—
*flop flop flop.*
"Max! Come out and play!" he
hollered.
But Max wasn't home.
He'd gone to visit his grandma.

He flopped over to Matthew's house—
*flop flop flop.*
"Matthew! Come out and play!"
But Matthew wasn't home, either.
He'd gone to play golf with his dad.

So he flopped over to Travis's house—
*flop flop flop.*
"Travis! Come out and play!"
But Travis wasn't home, either!
He'd gone to his tuba lesson.

Froggy dragged himself home—
*shlump shlump shlump.*

"Mom," cried Froggy. "Nobody's home."
"That's okay, dear," she said.
"I made a playdate for you. With Frogilina."
"No way!" cried Froggy.
"Yes way!" said Mom.
"Dad's taking you to the movies
to see *The Frog Prince*."

"I'M NOT GOING!" cried Froggy,
and he went to his room
and slammed the door—*BLAM!*

He plopped onto the bed
and blew his saxophone—
*honk! screeeech!*
*SQUAAAAAAWK!*

# FRROOGGYY!

yelled Dad.
"Wha-a-a-t?"
"STOP THAT RACKET!"

He blew once more—*BLEEEEEEP!*
Then he pulled on his baseball
glove and threw the ball against
the wall—
*thump  thump  thump!*

FRROOGGYY!

yelled Dad.
"Wha-a-a-t?"
"I told you to STOP THAT
RACKET! NOW!"

Froggy threw down his glove.
He wanted to go out and play,
but nobody was home.
And he did want to see
*The Frog Prince*.
(Even if Frogilina had to come along.)

So he hopped up
and put on his favorite bowtie—
*znap!*—
and looked at himself in the mirror.
"Hey, good lookin'!" he said, and
winked.

**FRROOGGYY!**

called Dad.
"Wha-a-a-a-t?"

"Let's go! It's time for your
playdate!"
"Wait!" said Froggy.
And he raced to the bathroom
and slapped on his dad's
aftershave—*splat splat splat*.
"Yikes!" he yelled. "My face
is on fire!"

When they got to Frogilina's,
she sniffed the air—*sniff sniff sniff.*
"Pee-yoo!" she said "What's that
funny smell?!"
"What smell?" said Froggy.
"I don't smell anything!"
And he hid behind his dad's back.

When they got to the movies,
Froggy sat with Dad in the dark.
Frogilina scooted next to Froggy

Froggy moved to the other side
of his dad.
But Frogilina moved next to him
again.
"Go away!" cried Froggy.
"Quiet!" said Dad. "The movie's
starting!"

It was hard to sit still.
Froggy tossed popcorn up
and tried to catch it in his mouth . . .

but some landed on Frogilina's head instead.
She threw a whole handful back.

"Popcorn fight!" cried Froggy.
Soon, there was a
blizzard of popcorn—
*zwit zwit zwit!*

"Stop it!" cried Dad.
"Sit still and watch the movie!"

"But I have to go to the bathroom!" cried Froggy. And Dad had to go with him.

By the time they got back,
Frogilina was watching her favorite part:
when the princess kisses the frog.
So what do you think she did?

She gave Froggy a big SMOOCH!
Smack on his cheek.

cried Froggy, looking more red in the face than green. "This is the worst playdate ever!"

On the way home from the movie, Froggy's dad got them ice cream cones at Screamin' Mimi's.

Froggy licked his—*sluuuurrrrp!*—and said,
"Want to taste mine?"
Frogilina batted her eyelashes and said,
"You're a real prince, Froggy!"

And she bit off the bottom half of his
cone—*crunch*—and handed it back

so ice cream dripped on Froggy's lap . . .

all the way home—*drip drip drip*.
It was the worst playdate ever!